Disney Princess Cookbook

RECIPES
Cynthia Littlefield, with additional recipes by Amy Croushorn,
Cristina Garces, and Joy Howard

PHOTOGRAPHY
Joanne Schmaltz, with additional photography by Joanna Chattman,
Teri Lyn Fisher, Amy Croushorn, Becky Sharp, and Jean Allsopp

FOOD STYLING
Edwina Stevenson, with additional styling by Amy Croushorn,
Joy Howard, and Jenny Park

ILLUSTRATIONS
Adrienne Brown and the Disney Storybook Art Team

DESIGN
Megan Youngquist

Printed in the United States of America
First Hardcover Edition, October 2013
Second Hardcover Edition, September 2021
3 5 7 9 10 8 6 4 2
Library of Congress Control Number: 2011943266
FAC-034274-21225
ISBN 978-1-368-06073-8
Visit www.disneybooks.com

Disney PRINCESS
Cookbook

Disney PRESS

Los Angeles • New York

Contents

Basics

Even though the Disney Princesses come from many different parts of the world—both land and sea—they all have a couple things in common: they inspire us to dream and to try new things! In this book, you'll find fifty yummy recipes inspired by Rapunzel, Tiana, Cinderella, and your other favorite princesses. Just turn the pages to discover delicious ideas for breakfast, lunch, and dinner, as well as tasty beverages, snacks, and desserts.

If you've never cooked before, don't worry! These dishes are perfect for beginner cooks. Remember that every recipe's difficulty is rated on a five-crown scale. That way, you can start by making something easy { 👑 } and work your way up to the most complicated recipes { 👑 👑 👑 👑 👑 }.

So grab your apron and get ready to cook up a royal feast!

Before You Begin

Cooking is a lot of fun, but before you get started, there are some important things to remember. Always, always ask a parent for permission. Even young princesses and princes need to check with the queen or king before they use the palace kitchen. If you need to use a stove, oven, blender, or mixer for a recipe, make sure to ask an adult to help you. Here are a few other tips to keep in mind.

- If you have long hair, tie it back. You don't want it to end up in the food or near a hot stove.

- Make sure your clothing isn't loose enough to touch a stovetop burner. If you're wearing long sleeves, push them up to your elbows.

- Put on an apron to keep your outfit from getting stained.

- Wash your hands with water and soap for at least twenty seconds so they will be clean when you handle the ingredients.

- Take a few minutes to read the whole recipe so that nothing will come as a surprise once you get started.

- Gather all the equipment you'll need, such as measuring spoons, bowls, baking pans, and utensils, before you get out the ingredients.

Measuring Ingredients

To make sure a recipe turns out just the way it's supposed to, you need to measure ingredients exactly. Here are some helpful hints and tips.

- For liquids like milk, water, or oil, use a measuring cup with a spout designed for pouring.

- A dry ingredient, such as flour, sugar, or cocoa, should be spooned into a measuring cup without a spout. Then, to check that you have the exact amount, scrape the flat edge of a butter knife across the rim of the cup to remove any extra.

- A chunky ingredient should be spooned into a measuring cup and then patted gently, just enough to even out the top without packing it down. Shredded ingredients are also measured this way.

- Brown sugar should be packed into measuring cups to press out any air bubbles.

- Measuring butter is really easy if you use sticks that have tablespoon marks printed on the wrapper. All you have to do is slice the butter where the line is.

Safety First!

A good cook never forgets that safety always comes first in the kitchen. Here are some important rules to follow.

Using knives, peelers, graters, and small kitchen appliances

- Never use a kitchen appliance or sharp utensil without asking an adult for help.

- Always use a cutting board when slicing or chopping ingredients. Grip the knife handle firmly, holding it so that the sharp edge is facing downward. Then slice through the ingredient, moving the knife away from yourself.

- After slicing raw meat or fish, wash the knife (with adult help) as well as the cutting board. You should also wash your hands with water and soap for at least twenty seconds before working with other ingredients.

- If you drop a knife, don't try to catch it. Instead, quickly step back and let the knife fall to the countertop or floor before picking it up by the handle.

- When using a vegetable peeler, press the edge of the blade into the vegetable's skin and then push the peeler away from yourself. Keep in mind that the more pressure you use, the thicker the peeling will be.

- Use electrical appliances, such as mixers and blenders, in a cleared space far away from the sink and other wet areas. And always unplug a mixer or blender before scraping a mixture from the beaters or blades.

Working around hot things

- Always ask an adult for help around a hot stovetop or oven.

- Make sure to point the handle of a stovetop pan away from you so you won't knock into it and accidentally tip the pot over.

- Use pot holders every time you touch a stovetop pot or skillet—even if it's just the lid. You should also use pot holders whenever you put a pan in the oven or take it out.

- Remember, steam can burn! Be sure to step back a bit when straining hot foods, such as pasta or cooked vegetables.

- Don't forget to shut off the oven or stove burner when the food is done baking or cooking.

Preparing Fruits and Vegetables

It's important to wash produce before adding it to a recipe. Here are some tips for making sure fruits and vegetables are clean and ready to use.

- Rinse produce well under plain running water. Don't use soap! If the produce is firm, like an apple or carrot, rub the surface to help remove any garden soil or grit. You can put softer fruits and vegetables, such as berries and broccoli florets, in a small colander or strainer before rinsing.

- Use a vegetable brush to scrub vegetables that grow underground, like potatoes and carrots. You should also scrub any fruits and vegetables that grow right on the ground, such as cucumbers and melons.

- Dry washed produce with a paper towel or reusable cleaning cloth and cut off any bruised parts before using it in a recipe.

Cleaning Up

A good cook always leaves the kitchen as tidy as they found it. This means cleaning all the bowls, pots, pans, and utensils you used to prepare the recipe. Here are some tips for making sure everything is spick-and-span.

- Always ask an adult for help washing knives and appliances with sharp blades, such as a blender or food processor.

- As you cook, try to give each bowl and utensil a quick rinse as soon as you're done with it. That way leftover food or batter won't stick to it before you can wash it with soap and water.

- Put all the ingredients back where they belong so you'll know just where to find them the next time you cook.

- Wipe down your work area—including the countertop and sink—with a damp paper towel or reusable cleaning cloth.

- Double-check that all the appliances you used are turned off before you leave the kitchen.

- Hang up your apron, or put it in the laundry if it needs to be washed.

Breakfast

Sunshine Bowl

Whether she's in her village of Motunui or sailing across the sea, Moana loves being in the sun. This sweet smoothie bowl, topped with fresh fruit and nuts, is the perfect way to bring some sunshine to your morning!

Directions

1. Place the coconut, banana, cantaloupe, Greek yogurt, and mandarin oranges into a blender.

2. Blend the ingredients until they are smooth and creamy.

3. Pour the smoothie into a bowl, add your preferred toppings, and serve with a spoon.

Serves 1

Ingredients

¼ cup shredded coconut

1 frozen banana

¼ cup frozen cantaloupe

½ cup Greek yogurt

2 mandarin oranges

Topping

Sliced almonds

Shredded coconut

Blueberries

Mandarin orange slices

Green grapes

Tip

To make this recipe your own, try experimenting with other fruits and nuts as your topping.

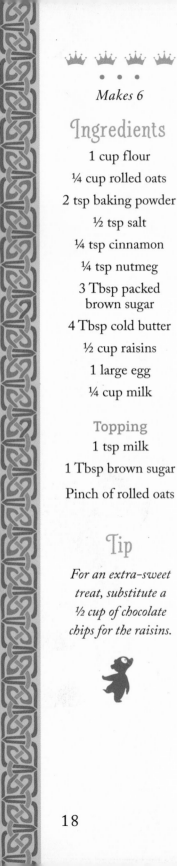

Ingredients

1 cup flour

¼ cup rolled oats

2 tsp baking powder

½ tsp salt

¼ tsp cinnamon

¼ tsp nutmeg

3 Tbsp packed
brown sugar

4 Tbsp cold butter

½ cup raisins

1 large egg

¼ cup milk

Topping

1 tsp milk

1 Tbsp brown sugar

Pinch of rolled oats

Tip

*For an extra-sweet
treat, substitute a
½ cup of chocolate
chips for the raisins.*

Scrumptious Scottish Scones

Merida loves grabbing treats at Castle DunBroch before
setting out to explore. These delicious Scottish scones, filled
with oats and raisins, are the perfect breakfast before a
fun-filled day of adventuring.

Directions

1. Heat the oven to 400°F.

2. In a large bowl, stir together the flour, rolled oats, baking
   powder, salt, cinnamon, nutmeg, and brown sugar. With a table
   knife, cut the butter into small pieces. Use your fingertips to
   pinch the butter into the flour until the lumps of butter are
   about the size of peas. Mix in the raisins.

3. In a small bowl, whisk the egg and milk together. Stir the egg
   mixture into the flour mixture until they are evenly combined.
   Be careful not to stir too long, or the scones will come out
   dense and heavy instead of fluffy.

4. Turn the dough onto a floured surface. Rub a little flour on your
   hands and pat the dough into a ¾-inch-thick circle.

5. Now make the topping. Use a pastry brush to spread a teaspoon
   of milk on the top of the dough. Sprinkle on the tablespoon of
   brown sugar and the pinch of rolled oats.

6. Cut the circle into 6 triangular pieces, just like you would cut
   a pie. Place the pieces slightly apart on an ungreased baking
   sheet.

7. Ask an adult to help you with the oven.
   Place the tray in the oven, and bake the scones
   until they start to turn golden brown
   (about 8 to 10 minutes).

8. Remove the tray from the oven.
   Let the scones cool
   for about 5 minutes
   before eating.

Good Morning Granola

Even on her busiest days as a maid, Cinderella brightened her mornings with a smile and a song. Brighten your day with this granola that takes only a few minutes to make.

Directions

1. Stir the granola and sunflower seeds together in a big bowl.

2. Choose the dried fruit you want to add. You can pick one or mix a few together. Add the fruit and almonds to the bowl.

3. Stir the granola until all the ingredients are well mixed. It's ready to eat right away

Serves 4 to 6

Ingredients

2 cups plain granola

¼ cup raw sunflower seeds

¼ cup dried fruit, such as chopped apricots, pineapple bits, cranberries, or raisins

¼ cup sliced almonds

Tip

Granola is more than just a breakfast cereal. It also tastes great mixed with yogurt or sprinkled on ice cream.

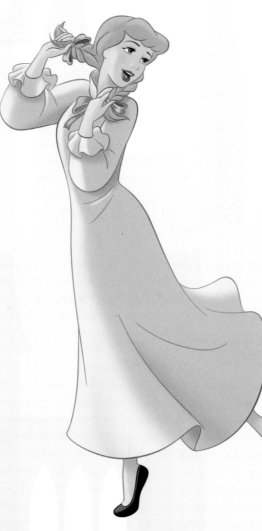

21

Ingredients

1 cup flour

½ cup brown sugar

1 tsp baking powder

¼ tsp cinnamon

¼ tsp salt

1 egg

½ cup milk

2 Tbsp butter, melted

½ cup blueberries

Serving Suggestion

Enjoy with a glass
of milk!

Tip

*For larger muffins,
just use a
12-cup muffin pan.
Then check the
muffins for doneness
after 15 to 18 minutes.*

Miners' Mini Muffins

Digging for diamonds is a full day's work. That's why the Seven Dwarfs always fuel up with a good breakfast before heading to the mines. And there's nothing like homemade mini muffins to start your day!

Directions

1. Heat the oven to 375°F. Lightly grease the bottom of a 24-cup mini muffin pan.

2. In a small mixing bowl, stir together the flour, brown sugar, baking powder, cinnamon, and salt.

3. In a bigger bowl, whisk together the egg, milk, and melted butter.

4. Stir the flour mixture into the egg mixture just until all the ingredients are wet. Use a rubber spatula to gently mix the blueberries into the batter.

5. Spoon the batter into the prepared pan until the muffin cups are about ⅔ full.

6. Ask an adult to help you with the oven. Place the muffin tray in the oven, and bake for about 12 minutes. You can tell if the muffins are done by sticking a toothpick into the center of one or two. If the toothpick comes out clean, the muffins are ready to take out.

7. Let the baked muffins cool in the pan for 2 or 3 minutes before turning them out on a cooling rack.

Frying Pan Eggs

It's no secret that Rapunzel knows how to use her frying pan. Make the frying pan your most trusted tool, too, by using it to whip up some eggs!

Directions

1. Crack the eggs into a small mixing bowl. Add the milk, salt, and pepper, and whisk all the ingredients together.

2. Ask an adult to help you at the stove. Melt the butter in a skillet over low heat, then pour in the egg mixture.

3. Sprinkle 2 tablespoons of add-ins on top of the eggs.

4. Use a spatula to push the cooking eggs into the center of the pan, allowing the still-liquid egg to flow in underneath. Repeat until there's no liquid left and the eggs are cooked through (about 3 to 4 minutes).

Serves 2

Ingredients

2 large eggs

2 Tbsp milk

Salt and pepper to taste

⅓ Tbsp butter

2 Tbsp of add-ins from the list below

Add-In Choices

Shredded cheddar cheese

Bacon bits

Diced ham

Diced cooked potatoes

Diced red bell pepper

Diced tomato

Spinach

Salsa

Tip

For scrambled eggs that are soft and fluffy, whisk the mixture an extra minute or two before pouring it in the pan.

Smiling Breakfast Bowl

On Mulan's first day of training, she wakes up and eats a piping hot bowl of porridge adorned with a smiling face. Re-create the scene with your own version.

Ingredients

1 cup prepared hot cereal (such as oatmeal or cream of wheat.)

Half a peach, canned or fresh, peeled

3 Tbsp plain Greek yogurt

1 slice cooked bacon

Directions

1. Prepare the hot cereal according to the directions on the box. Place the cereal in a bowl.

2. With help from an adult, use a mini round cutter to shape two circles from the peach half. Spoon two yogurt eyes on top of the cereal, as shown, then top each with a peach center. Finish with a bacon strip mouth. Serve immediately.

Tip

There's more than one way to make a smile! Try substituting other types of fruit or yogurt into the recipe, too.

Baked Caramel French Toast

This sweet French toast dish makes enough for a big group to enjoy! Share this with family and friends, and you'll feel like you're dining out together at Tiana's Palace.

Directions

1. Generously butter a 9 × 13-inch casserole dish. Place the bread pieces in the dish.

2. In a small bowl, mix together the brown sugar, cinnamon, and salt. Sprinkle the mixture over the bread.

3. In a mixing bowl, whisk together the eggs, milk, and vanilla extract. Pour the egg mixture evenly over the bread. Then use a spatula to press the bread down to make sure it is well coated.

4. Cover the baking pan with aluminum foil and refrigerate it for at least 4 hours, or overnight.

5. When you're ready to cook the French toast, heat the oven to 350°F. Ask an adult to help you with the oven. Bake the French toast with the foil in place for 20 minutes. Remove the foil, and continue baking for another 25 minutes.

6. Take the tray out of the oven and let cool for about 5 minutes before serving.

Serves 8 to 10

Ingredients

Small (10-oz) loaf of French bread, pulled apart into 1-inch pieces

⅓ cup brown sugar

¾ tsp cinnamon

Dash of salt

6 large eggs

1¼ cups milk

1 tsp vanilla extract

Tip

To change it up, try using a loaf of raisin bread instead of French bread.

Lunch

Castle Corn Chowder

♕ ♕ ♕
• • •

Serves 4 to 6

Ingredients

1 medium onion

2 medium red potatoes

2 Tbsp butter

1 cup water

2 cups whole-kernel corn

1½ cups creamed corn

1½ cups milk

Salt and pepper to taste

5 Tbsp bacon bit

Tip

*Try this soup with
a Bonjour Baguette (p. 74)
for a delicious
combination.*

Belle and the Beast love having snowball fights in the courtyard—and warming up inside afterward! This corn chowder tastes even better after a chilly day outside.

Directions

1. Peel off the onion's hard outer layer, and cut the onion into ½-inch pieces. Then chop the red potatoes into bite-size cubes. Set the onion and potatoes aside.

2. Ask an adult to help you at the stove. Melt the butter in a heavy saucepan over medium-low heat. Cook the onion in the melted butter until the onion starts to turn clear (about 3 or 4 minutes).

3. Add the potatoes and water, then cover the pan and let simmer for 15 minutes.

4. Stir in the whole-kernel corn, creamed corn, milk, salt, and pepper. Continue cooking and stirring the chowder until it heats through (about 7 minutes).

5. Ladle the chowder into bowls, sprinkle bacon bits on top, and serve.

Sweet Dough Turnovers

Tiana loves discovering her friends' favorite foods. These turnovers are perfect for sharing with all sorts of eaters—you can try them with the more traditional sweet potato filling, or a broccoli and cheese filling, or create your own custom versions.

Directions

1. In a small bowl, whisk together the flour, baking powder, and salt, and set aside.

2. Using a handheld mixer, cream together the butter and sugar until the mixture is light and fluffy, about 3 minutes. Add the vanilla and the egg and mix to combine. Alternate mixing in a little of the flour mixture with a little of the milk until both are combined. Transfer the dough to a sheet of plastic wrap, roll it up, and place it in the refrigerator for 15 minutes.

3. Preheat the oven to 375°F. Combine the ingredients for your preferred filling in a small bowl. Remove the dough from the refrigerator and separate into 4 pieces. On a floured surface, roll the dough out into 4 circles with a rolling pin. You can use the mouth of a small bowl to cut out perfect circles, or leave them as they are for a more homemade look.

4. Using a spoon, scoop a fourth of the filling into the center of each small circle. Add water to the edges of the dough, fold the circle in half, and crimp the edges together with a fork.

5. Ask an adult for help with the oven. Place on a baking sheet, and bake for 12 to 15 minutes or until golden brown on the outside. Once the turnovers are done, make sure to let them cool down before taking a bite!

Makes 4

Ingredients

Sweet Dough

1 cup plus 2 Tbsp all-purpose flour

½ tsp baking powder

¼ tsp salt

3 Tbsp unsalted butter, softened

1 Tbsp sugar

¼ tsp vanilla extract

1 Tbsp beaten egg

2 Tbsp milk

Sweet Potato Filling

1 (15-oz) can yams in syrup, drained and mashed

¼ tsp cinnamon

¼ tsp nutmeg

¼ tsp ginger

Broccoli and Cheese Filling

1 cup broccoli, cooked

½ cup cheddar cheese, shredded

1 cup cooked chicken or ham, cubed (optional)

35

Ingredients

2 cups flour

½ cup cornmeal

3 tsp baking powder

1 tsp salt

5 Tbsp cold butter, cut into several pieces

½ cup diced ham

½ cup shredded cheddar cheese

1 cup milk

Tip

You can use grated Parmesan or Romano cheese instead of cheddar, if you'd like.

Ham and Cheese Biscuit Braids

Rapunzel loves to wear her long hair in beautiful braids while she paints and draws. Practice your own braiding skills with these uniquely shaped biscuits!

Directions

1. Heat the oven to 400°F.

2. In a mixing bowl, stir together the flour, cornmeal, baking powder, and salt.

3. Use your fingertips to pinch the butter into the flour mixture until the bits are the size of peas. Stir in the ham and cheese. Add the milk, and stir the mixture just until it starts to look doughy.

4. Sprinkle some flour onto a cutting board and set the dough on top. Sprinkle a little more flour on the dough to keep it from sticking. Using a rolling pin, flatten the dough into a 12-inch square. The dough should be between ¼ inch and ½ inch thick.

5. Slice the square into quarters. Then slice each quarter into 12 strips, each about 6 inches long.

6. Now it's time to braid the dough. Gather 3 strips, and pinch them together at the top. Take the right section and cross it over the center section so that they switch places. Then, take the left section and cross it over the center section. Keep going until the whole strip is braided, then pinch the strands together at the bottom. Repeat until you've braided all the strips.

7. Ask an adult to help you with the oven. Place the braids, spaced apart, on an ungreased baking sheet. Bake them until the dough starts to turn golden brown (about 8 to 10 minutes).

Magic Carpet Roll-Ups

Brightly trimmed with carrot and red-pepper tassels, these roll-up sandwiches are shaped like Jasmine's friend the Magic Carpet—and make for a perfect lunch on the fly.

Directions

1. Ask an adult to help you prepare the vegetables. Peel the carrot and slice it into 3-inch-long sections. Cut each section into thin strips. Slice the red bell pepper into similarly sized strips.

2. Trim off the curved edges of each flatbread or tortilla to create a rectangular "carpet" shape.

3. Spread cream cheese on the surface of each flatbread, and then roll it up.

4. Add "tassels" to each Magic Carpet sandwich by inserting several of the carrot and red-pepper strips into the center coil at both ends.

Makes 2

Ingredients

1 carrot

Half of a red bell pepper

2 flatbreads or large flour tortillas

Cream cheese spread (plain or veggie)

Tip

You can make these roll-ups using hummus instead of cream cheese. Try Wondrous Homemade Hummus on p. 90!

Tasty Flower Sandwiches

Living near the Louisiana bayou, Tiana and Naveen are never too far from the great outdoors. Bring a bit of nature to lunchtime with these flower-shaped sandwiches!

Directions

1. In a small bowl, stir together the mayonnaise, garlic powder, and paprika.

2. For each sandwich, use a large flower-shaped cookie cutter (about 3 inches wide) to cut the center from a slice of white bread. Next, cut a matching flower shape from a slice of wheat bread.

3. Use a small round cookie cutter (about 1¼ inches wide) to cut a hole in the middle of each bread flower cutout. Place the center of the wheat flower into the white flower and the center of the white flower into the wheat flower.

4. Cut flower shapes from slices of ham and cheese (but don't cut holes in the centers).

5. Spread mayonnaise mixture on one of the bread flowers, and layer on the ham and cheese cutouts. Top off the sandwich with the second bread flower. You can spread a little more mayonnaise on this layer, too, if you'd like.

Seven Dwarfs Soup

Made with seven tasty ingredients—one for each of the dwarfs—this recipe adds up to one delicious meal. Careful! The pepper might make you Sneezy. . . .

Directions

1. Peel the carrot and cut it into thin slices. Prepare your celery stalks by slicing off the leafy tops and white bottoms. Cut the remaining stalks into thin slices.

2. Ask an adult to help you combine the chicken broth, carrot slices, and celery slices in a large saucepan. Cook over high heat until the broth begins to bubble. Turn the heat down to low and let simmer for 3 minutes.

3. Stir in the chicken and pasta. Continue simmering the soup until the pasta is cooked al dente (about 10 more minutes).

4. Season the soup with salt and ground pepper, and serve.

Serves 3 to 4

Ingredients

1 carrot

2 stalks celery

1 qt chicken broth

1 cooked chicken breast, cut into small pieces (about 1 packed cup)

½ cup uncooked ditalini or similar pasta

Salt and pepper to taste

Tip

For a simpler soup, bring the broth to a simmer and stir in 1 cup frozen mixed vegetables in place of the carrot and celery.

Ingredients

16 oz premade
pizza dough

1 Tbsp olive oil

2 pinches cornmeal

1 cup pizza sauce

1½ cups grated
mozzarella cheese

Toppings

Diced ham

Pepperoni

Broccoli florets

Diced bell peppers

Pineapple chunks

Sliced black olives

Tip

*If you use pineapple
chunks for a topping,
blot them first with a
paper towel or clean
reusable cloth to absorb
extra juice and keep
the crust from
getting soggy.*

Bull's-Eye Pizza

Nothing's more important to Princess Merida than being able
to make her own choices. That's why this pizza recipe is all
about targeting the toppings you like best.

Directions

1. Divide the pizza dough in half and knead each piece into a
   ball. Place the dough balls in a large bowl and cover with
   plastic wrap. Let them rest at room temperature for 10 minutes.

2. Heat the oven to 425°F. Lightly oil two baking sheets and
   sprinkle a pinch or two of cornmeal on top.

3. Working on a flour-dusted surface, roll both dough balls into
   ¼-inch-thick circles. Carefully place each one on a prepared
   baking sheet.

4. Spread spoonfuls of pizza sauce on both pizza crusts. Top the
   sauce with grated mozzarella cheese.

5. Add your choice of toppings. Place one kind—chopped ham or
   pepperoni slices, for example—in the center. Arrange a second
   topping in a ring around the first one. Keep adding toppings in
   this way, creating a colorful bull's-eye pattern, until you reach
   the crust.

6. Ask an adult to help you with the oven. Bake the pizzas on
   different oven racks until the edges and bottoms of the crusts
   are golden brown (about 15 minutes). Switch the position
   of the trays after 7 or 8 minutes so that the pizzas will cook
   evenly.

7. Let the cooked pizzas cool
   slightly before slicing
   and serving.

Pumpkin Hazelnut Soup

Hazelnut soup often cheered Rapunzel up when she lived in her tower. Try this delicious, unique pumpkin spin on the dish when you need an afternoon boost!

Directions

1. Have an adult help you warm the olive oil in a large pot over medium heat. Once the oil begins to simmer, add the shallot and salt. Cook, stirring occasionally, until the shallot becomes tender and translucent, about 7 to 8 minutes.

2. Add the chicken or vegetable stock, applesauce, pepper, nutmeg, pumpkin puree, and brown sugar, and simmer for 15 minutes. Add the sour cream and stir to combine.

3. With an adult's help, heat the oil in a small pan over medium heat and add the bread crumbs. Stir them around until they're crisp and golden, about 3 minutes. Pour in the hazelnuts, and toast everything together for 2 minutes. Top each bowl of soup with a tablespoon of bread crumb topping.

Serves 4 to 6

Ingredients

Pumpkin Soup

1 Tbsp olive oil

1 shallot, diced

½ tsp salt

3 cups chicken or vegetable stock

1 cup unsweetened applesauce

¼ tsp pepper

⅛ tsp nutmeg

1 (15-oz) can pumpkin puree

2 Tbsp brown sugar

½ cup sour cream

Hazelnut Bread Topping

½ Tbsp olive oil

¼ cup panko bread crumbs

¼ cup hazelnuts, chopped

Dinner

Ingredients

1 cup butter cracker crumbs

⅓ cup grated Parmesan cheese

½ tsp garlic powder

½ tsp paprika

¼ tsp salt

¼ tsp ground pepper

2 eggs

2 Tbsp water

1 Tbsp honey

1½ lb skinless chicken tenders

Tip

Serve your chicken tenders with honey mustard or barbecue sauce for dipping.

Cozy Cottage Chicken Tenders

The fairies who took Aurora in were never very good at cooking. . . . Luckily, this chicken tenders recipe is so easy that you don't need a magic wand to prepare it.

Directions

1. Heat the oven to 400°F. Line a baking sheet with parchment paper.

2. Combine the cracker crumbs, Parmesan, garlic powder, paprika, salt, and pepper in a sealable gallon-size plastic bag.

3. In a medium-size bowl, whisk together the eggs, water, and honey.

4. Pat the chicken tenders dry with paper towels or a clean reusable cloth. Place the tenders in the egg mixture so that they are completely covered.

5. Use a fork to transfer 2 or 3 tenders to the bag of cracker crumbs. Seal the bag, and shake. Arrange the coated chicken pieces on the baking sheet. Repeat this step until all the tenders are coated and on the sheet.

6. Ask an adult to help you with the oven. Bake the chicken for 10 minutes. Then turn the pieces over and continue baking until they are cooked through (another 10 minutes or so).

Hoppin' John

Tiana puts food on her restaurant menu that can be enjoyed year-round. But sometimes, dishes can make holidays extra special! This popular Southern dish is supposed to bring good luck if you eat it on New Year's Day.

Directions

1. Rinse the black-eyed peas in a metal strainer, then put them in a large saucepan.

2. Ask an adult for help at the stove. Pour in 4 cups of the water. Bring the black-eyed peas to a boil and cook them for 2 minutes. Then remove the pan from the heat and let the black-eyed peas stand for 1 hour.

3. Melt the butter in a large skillet over low heat. Add the ham, onion, celery, carrots, garlic, celery salt, red pepper flakes, and pepper. Cook the mixture until it heats through and the onion starts to look clear (about 6 to 8 minutes).

4. Add the black-eyed peas and their liquid to the skillet and stir. Bring the mixture to a boil, and then lower the heat until the cooking slows down to a simmer. Cover the pan and continue cooking until the beans are tender, about 6 to 8 minutes.

5. Pour in 1 more cup of water, and stir in the rice. Re-cover the skillet and continue simmering for about 20 minutes, or until the rice is cooked.

6. Drain off any extra liquid, give the Hoppin' John a final stir, and serve.

Serves 6 to 8

Ingredients

½ lb dried black-eyed peas

4 cups water

1 Tbsp butter

½ lb baked ham, cubed

1 medium onion, chopped

2 stalks celery, chopped

2 medium carrots, chopped

2 cloves garlic, minced

¼ tsp celery salt

¼ tsp red pepper flakes

Dash of pepper

1 cup water

1 cup long grain white rice

Tip

When you rinse the black-eyed peas, be sure to sort through them for any loose pebbles that might have been mixed in by mistake when they were picked.

53

Ingredients

1 egg

1½ cups flaked cooked
cod fillets (about 12 oz)

5 Tbsp Italian-style
bread crumbs

2 Tbsp mayonnaise

1 Tbsp lime juice

¼ tsp paprika

¼ tsp celery salt

Dash of pepper

3 tsp vegetable oil

½ tsp butter

Tip

*Make your own yummy
dipping sauce by stirring
a little lime juice and
a dash of celery salt into
a large spoonful
of mayonnaise.*

Unbearably Delicious Fish Cakes

Fish will always remind Merida and her mum, Queen Elinor, of their adventure together. These fish cakes are perfect for when you're as hungry as a bear, too!

Directions

1. In a large bowl, crack the egg and beat it with a whisk.

2. Break up the cod fillets into bite-size pieces, and mix with the eggs. Then add the bread crumbs, mayonnaise, lime juice, paprika, celery salt, and pepper. Mix well with a rubber spatula.

3. Cover the bowl with plastic wrap and chill for 15 minutes in the refrigerator.

4. Ask an adult for help at the stove. Heat the vegetable oil and butter in a frying pan on medium low. When the butter starts to bubble, spoon six equal mounds of the fish cake mixture into the pan. Press down on them lightly with the back of the spoon to flatten the tops.

5. Cook the fish cakes for 3 to 4 minutes on each side, then serve.

Mac and Cheeseburger

This saucy supper features Gus the mouse's favorite snack: cheese! Combined with bite-size bits of burger and a buttery cracker topping, this flavorful dish is a dream come true.

Directions

1. Ask an adult to help you at the stove. Cook the macaroni according to the directions on the box.

2. Place the ground beef or turkey in a heavy saucepan and cook over medium heat. Make sure to cook the meat until it is completely brown, then drain off any liquid.

3. Heat the oven to 350°F. Combine the hamburger and the cooked macaroni in a 2½- or 3-quart casserole dish.

4. Melt the 4 tablespoons of butter in a heavy saucepan over medium heat. Stir the flour into the butter with a wooden spoon. As soon as the sauce starts to bubble, add the milk, mustard, and nutmeg, and whisk until the mixture is blended.

5. Stir in the cheese, and continue stirring until it is completely melted and the sauce starts to thicken.

6. Ladle the cheese sauce into the casserole dish, and gently stir until the macaroni and hamburger are evenly coated.

7. Mix all the topping ingredients together in a bowl and then sprinkle them on the macaroni.

8. Ask an adult to help you with the oven. Put the casserole dish in the oven. Bake the macaroni and cheese until it heats all the way through and starts to bubble (about 20 to 25 minutes). Let cool slightly before serving.

Serves 4 to 6

Ingredients

1 (16-oz) box of elbow macaroni

½ lb ground beef or turkey (85% to 90% lean)

4 Tbsp butter

3 Tbsp flour

2½ cups milk

1 Tbsp mustard

Dash of nutmeg

4 cups shredded sharp cheddar cheese

Topping

2 Tbsp butter, melted

½ cup bread crumbs or cracker crumbs

⅛ tsp paprika

Tip

Get creative! Try mixing and matching different kinds of cheese for this recipe

Bayou Meatloaf

The creatures of the bayou can't make music on empty stomachs! This hearty meatloaf is a showstopper, just like Louis's trumpet playing.

Ingredients

1 lb ground beef
or turkey
(85% to 90% lean)

1 lb ground pork

1 tsp celery salt

1 tsp garlic powder

1 tsp dried thyme

1 tsp paprika

¼ tsp pepper

1 cup bread crumbs

½ cup minced onion

½ cup ketchup

½ cup milk

2 large eggs, lightly
beaten

Topping

½ cup ketchup with
1 Tbsp honey stirred in

Tip

Leftover meatloaf tastes great in a sandwich, especially if you toast the bread.

Directions

1. Heat the oven to 350°F. Grease the bottom and sides of a 2½-quart casserole dish.

2. Combine the ground beef or turkey and ground pork in a large mixing bowl.

3. In a small bowl or cup, stir together the celery salt, garlic powder, thyme, paprika, and pepper. Sprinkle the mixture over the meat.

4. Add the bread crumbs, onion, ketchup, milk, and eggs to the meat. Use a wooden spoon to stir all the ingredients together until they are well mixed. Pack the meatloaf mixture into the casserole dish.

5. Ask an adult to help you with the oven. Place the meatloaf in the oven and bake for 50 minutes. Then carefully remove it from the oven. Spread the ketchup and honey mixture on top using a spoon or spatula. Return the meatloaf to the oven to bake for 10 more minutes.

6. Let the meatloaf cool for a few minutes before you slice and serve it.

Beastly Quiche

When Belle met the Beast, she taught him all sorts of new things—like how to eat with a fork! Show off your own table manners by dining on this quiche.

Directions

1. Heat the oven to 425°F.

2. Set the pie shell in its pan on a heavy baking sheet. (This will make it easier to move once you fill it.) Loosely cover the outer edge of the pie shell with strips of aluminum foil to keep it from browning too quickly in the oven.

3. Sprinkle the cheese evenly across the bottom of the pie shell. Add the crumbled bacon and broccoli florets.

4. In a large mixing bowl, whisk together the eggs, milk, and pepper until they are well mixed. Pour the mixture over the other ingredients in the pie shell.

5. Ask an adult to help you with the oven. Bake the quiche for 15 minutes. Then reduce the heat to 325°F. Carefully remove the aluminum foil from the edge of the shell, and continue baking for 25 minutes.

6. Let the quiche cool slightly before serving.

Serves 6 to 8

Ingredients

Premade frozen 9-inch pie shell

1 cup grated cheddar cheese

4 strips cooked bacon, crumbled

1 cup cooked broccoli florets

4 eggs

1 cup milk

¼ tsp pepper

Tip

You can eat quiche anytime—for breakfast, lunch, or dinner!

Serves 6 to 8

Ingredients

2 Tbsp butter

1 medium onion, chopped

1 stalk celery, chopped

1½ lb ground beef

¼ tsp garlic powder

3 Tbsp flour

1 cup beef broth

1 (14.5-oz) can
diced tomatoes

1 tsp dried thyme

½ tsp dried rosemary

1½ cups corn kernels

5 cups warm
mashed potatoes

Paprika

Tip

*It takes about
6 medium-large
potatoes to make
5 cups of mashed
potatoes.*

Savory Shepherd's Pie

If you want to go on new adventures every day like Merida, don't miss this filling dish—it will fill both your belly and your heart.

Directions

1. Heat the oven to 400°F. Ask an adult to help you at the stove. Melt the butter in a large frying pan over medium heat. Add the onion and celery, and sauté them for 5 minutes, stirring often.

2. Add the ground beef to the pan, and break it up with a wooden spoon or spatula. Cook the meat, stirring and turning it over every so often, until it browns. Then lower the heat, and carefully spoon out any excess fat from the cooking liquid.

3. Stir the garlic powder and flour into the beef. Add the beef broth, diced tomatoes, thyme, rosemary, and corn. Gently stir all the ingredients until they are well combined.

4. Bring the mixture to a simmer, and cook for 3 or 4 minutes. Then spoon it into a large greased casserole dish.

5. Spread the warm mashed potatoes on top of the meat and corn. Sprinkle the top with paprika.

6. Ask an adult to help you with the oven. Bake the shepherd's pie until it heats all the way through and the top turns golden brown (about 25 minutes). Let cool for 10 minutes before serving.

Sides

Lucky Cucumber Salad

Mulan's cricket friend, Cri-Kee, loves spending time in the Fa family garden. Make your own lucky salad dish with some crunchy cucumbers!

Directions

1. Cut the cucumber into thin circular slices.

2. In a medium-size bowl, stir together the cucumber slices, vinegar, sugar, sesame seeds, and salt. Add the crushed red pepper flakes if you're using them.

3. Chill the cucumber salad for 30 minutes before serving.

Serves 6 to 8

Ingredients

1 medium English cucumber

3 Tbsp rice vinegar

1 Tbsp sugar

1 Tbsp toasted sesame seeds

Salt to taste

Dash of crushed red pepper flakes (optional)

Tip

Red pepper flakes are really spicy, so don't use too many.

Ingredients

1 (16-oz) box of pasta shells

½ cup diced red bell pepper

½ cup shredded carrots

½ cup halved cherry tomatoes

¼ cup grated Parmesan cheese

2 Tbsp snipped chives

1 cup Italian salad dressing

Salt and pepper to taste

Tip

Cubed mozzarella cheese and pepperoni slices make great additions to this salad.

Pasta Shell Salad

Ariel loves both land and sea. This colorful combination of garden veggies and shell-shaped pasta is the perfect mix of her two worlds.

Directions

1. Ask an adult for help at the stove. Prepare the pasta according to the directions on the box.

2. In a large bowl, combine the cooked pasta shells, red pepper, carrots, cherry tomatoes, Parmesan, and chives. Stir with a wooden spoon to mix them.

3. Pour the Italian salad dressing over the pasta, and sprinkle on the salt and pepper. Stir again until all the ingredients are evenly coated.

4. Cover the bowl with plastic wrap and chill until serving time.

Sweet Potato Coins

These sweet and salty oven fries resemble the golden coins found in the Cave of Wonders. But these coins are much tastier!

Directions

1. Heat the oven to 400°F. Use a small round cookie cutter (up to 2 inches wide or so) to cut out a bunch of "coins" from the sweet potato slices. To make cutting through the slices extra easy, place the flat end of a wooden spoon on top of the cutter, and press down on the spoon.

2. Put the potato coins in a mixing bowl. Drizzle the oil on top, and stir with a wooden spoon until the coins are evenly coated.

3. Line a baking sheet with aluminum foil. Then, place the coins on the sheet, spacing them slightly apart. Sprinkle on salt and pepper.

4. Ask an adult to help you with the oven. Bake the coins until the bottoms are golden brown, about 10 to 12 minutes. Remove them from the oven, and use a spatula to flip them over. Bake the coins for another 10 to 12 minutes.

Serves 2 to 3

Ingredients

2 medium-size sweet potatoes, peeled and sliced about ¼ inch thick

1 Tbsp vegetable oil or olive oil

Salt and pepper to taste

Tip

You can use different cookie cutters, such as stars or hearts, to make fun shapes, too!

Southern Spoon Bread

♛ ♛ ♛ ♛
• • •

Serves 6 to 8

Ingredients

2 cups milk

1 cup water

1 Tbsp butter

1 tsp salt

1 cup cornmeal

2 eggs

2 Tbsp honey

2½ tsp baking powder

Tip

Not sure how to separate egg whites and yolks? Check out the glossary (p. 136)!

At her restaurant, Tiana serves unique versions of her favorite dishes. Put your own spin on a side dish with this spoon bread recipe. It tastes a lot like cornbread, but it has a delicious gooey texture that's fun to spoon up at mealtime.

Directions

1. Heat the oven to 375°. Butter a 2-quart casserole dish.

2. Ask an adult to help you at the stove. Heat the milk and water in a large heavy saucepan over medium heat. Turn the heat to low as soon as bubbles form against the pan (before the milk boils). Add the butter and salt, and stir until the butter melts.

3. Slowly whisk the cornmeal into the milk. Keep whisking just until the mixture thickens (about 1 minute). Remove the pan from the heat and let the cornmeal cool a bit.

4. Separate the egg yolks and the egg whites into different mixing bowls.

5. Beat the egg whites with a mixer until they are foamy and stiff, and set them aside.

6. Beat together the yolks, honey, and baking powder with a fork or whisk. Then whisk the mixture into the cornmeal. Pour the cornmeal mixture into the bowl of beaten egg whites.

7. Use a rubber spatula to gently fold the egg whites into the cornmeal.

8. Scrape the spoon bread batter into the casserole dish. Ask an adult to help you put the dish in the oven. Bake it until the top turns golden brown and a toothpick inserted in the middle comes out clean (about 25 to 30 minutes). Serve the spoon bread warm, scooping it out of the casserole dish with a big spoon.

Bonjour Baguette

One of Belle's favorite shops is the bakery. The best time to get there is bright and early, when the baker first takes the fresh baguettes out of the oven.

Directions

1. Pour the ½ cup of warm water into a mixing bowl, and sprinkle the yeast on top. Once the yeast dissolves, stir in the 1½ cups of water, the salt, and 4 cups of the flour.

2. Sprinkle the remaining ½ cup of flour onto a cutting board, and turn the dough out onto it. Knead the dough until all the flour is mixed in. Put the dough in a greased bowl, and cover it with a damp paper towel. Set the bowl aside in a warm spot until the dough doubles in size (about 1 hour).

3. Sprinkle the cornmeal onto a large baking sheet. Punch down the dough and then divide it into halves. Shape each half into a 12-inch-long fat rope, and place them on the baking sheet.

4. Cut a few ¼-inch-deep diagonal slits in the top of each loaf. Cover the bread with damp paper towels, and set it aside to rise for 1 hour.

5. Heat the oven to 400°F. Use a pastry brush to lightly brush the top of each loaf with milk. Ask an adult to help you place the pan in the oven. Bake the bread until it turns golden brown, 20 to 25 minutes.

Makes 2

Ingredients

½ cup warm water

1 package active dry yeast

1½ cups water
(at room temperature)

1½ tsp salt

4½ cups flour

2 Tbsp cornmeal

1 Tbsp milk

Tip

*Try this bread as
a side for
Castle Corn Chowder
(p. 32)!*

Ingredients

Half of a cantaloupe

Half of a
honeydew melon

Half of a small seedless
watermelon

Tip

*This summertime
salad is even more
refreshing when served
with snipped mint.*

Triple-licious Fruit Salad

Just like Merida's brothers, Harris, Hubert, and Hamish, this sweet and juicy tricolored treat proves that groups of three can be lots of fun.

Directions

1. Use a melon baller to scoop 1 dozen balls from each melon half, and combine them all in a big bowl.

2. Gently stir the melon balls with a wooden spoon so that the colors are evenly mixed.

3. Spoon your fruit salad into small serving dishes, and enjoy! Cover any leftover fruit salad with plastic wrap, and chill it in the refrigerator until you're ready for more.

All-Dressed-Up Salad

Cinderella's fairy godmother can transform a pumpkin into a coach, mice into horses, and rags into a beautiful dress. You can create magic of your own by turning a few simple ingredients into an amazing salad dressing.

Directions

1. Rinse the lettuce well with cold water, and then pat the leaves dry with paper towels. Tear the lettuce into bite-size pieces and put an equal amount on 3 salad plates.

2. Top the lettuce on each plate with ⅓ cup shredded carrot, 5 cucumber slices, and 3 cherry tomatoes.

3. In a small bowl, whisk together the orange juice, lemon juice, vegetable oil, and honey.

4. Spoon dressing onto each salad, and serve.

Serves 3

Ingredients

1 head of lettuce

1 cup shredded carrot

15 cucumber slices

9 cherry tomatoes, halved

Citrus Dressing

½ cup orange juice

2 Tbsp lemon juice

1 Tbsp vegetable oil

1 Tbsp honey

Tip

Sweeten up your salad by sprinkling sliced almonds and fresh fruit on top.

Serves 6

Ingredients

1 tsp vegetable oil

½ cup diced
red bell pepper

2 cups cooked corn

1 tsp dried basil

½ tsp butter

Salt and pepper to taste

3 strips cooked
bacon, crumbled
(optional)

Tip

*Leftover cooked
sweet corn, cut off the
cob, tastes especially
good in this recipe.*

Confetti Corn

Made with red pepper, yellow corn, and green basil, this colorful medley is as festive as a music-filled night at Tiana's Palace.

Directions

1. Ask an adult to help you at the stove. Heat the vegetable oil in a medium-size frying pan over medium-low heat. Sauté the diced red pepper in the oil for 2 minutes.

2. Add the corn, basil, butter, and bacon (if using). Stir the ingredients together, and cook them until they are hot and well mixed and the butter is melted.

3. Remove the pan from the heat. Stir in salt and pepper to taste.

Dinglehopper Snow Peas

Ariel loves to use her dinglehopper—what humans call a fork. Use your own dinglehopper to eat these deliciously crunchy veggies.

Directions

1. Rinse the snow peas well in cold water. Then snap off the top of each pod, pulling it downward to remove the strings along the sides.

2. Place the prepared pods and the tablespoon of water in a microwavable casserole dish. Cover the dish, and microwave the peas on high for 3 minutes.

3. Use pot holders to remove the casserole dish from the microwave. Add butter to the peas, gently stir, and serve.

Serves 3 to 4

Ingredients

½ lb snow peas

1 Tbsp water

1 tsp butter

Tip

For a zestier dish, drizzle ½ teaspoon or so of Italian dressing on the snow peas instead of butter.

Snacks

Ingredients

1 cup whipped
cream cheese

1 cup sour cream

2 tsp dried dill weed

1 Tbsp garlic powder

¼ tsp salt

Baby carrots

Tip

*This dip tastes great
with celery, too!*

Chomptastic Carrots and Dip

Maximus enjoys snacks that have a good crunch to them. This carrots-and-dip combo will delight your chompers, too.

Directions

1. In a medium-size bowl, stir together the whipped cream cheese and sour cream until well blended. Then stir in the dill weed, garlic powder, and salt.

2. Chill the dip for at least 30 minutes. Serve it with plenty of baby carrots.

Under-the-Sea Sand Dollar Crackers

Ariel collects all sorts of treasures from the human world! Bake your own treasures with these homemade crackers inspired by beautiful sand dollars you might find on the beach.

Directions

1. Heat the oven to 400°F. Line a large baking sheet with parchment paper.

2. In a mixing bowl, whisk together the flour, Parmesan cheese, salt, and paprika. Add the butter pieces to the flour mixture, and use your fingers to pinch them until the bits are the size of small peas.

3. Add the half-and-half and stir until the dough pulls together. Turn the dough onto a lightly floured surface, and knead it a few times.

4. Use a floured rolling pin to roll the cracker dough very thin (about ⅛ inch thick). With a round cookie cutter (about 2¼ inches wide), cut out a bunch of circles from the dough. Arrange the dough circles, spaced apart, on the baking sheet. Gather the dough scraps and knead them together, then reroll the dough so you can cut more circles from it.

5. Use the tip of a toothpick or wooden kitchen skewer to poke through the center of each dough circle, and wiggle it around to make a small hole. This helps keep the cracker flat when it bakes.

6. Working with one cracker at a time, use a pastry brush to spread a tiny bit of water on top. Then lightly press 5 almond slices into the dough around the hole to create a star shape.

7. Ask an adult to help you with the oven. Bake the crackers until they start to brown on top, about 6 to 7 minutes. Remove them from the oven and transfer them to a wire rack to cool for a bit before you eat them.

Makes 4 dozen

Ingredients

1¼ cups flour

⅓ cup grated Parmesan cheese

½ tsp salt

½ tsp paprika

3 Tbsp cold butter, cut into pieces

½ cup half-and-half

Sliced almonds

Tip

If you want to make the crackers without almonds, you can simply use a toothpick to poke a sand dollar pattern in the dough.

Ingredients

1 (15-oz) can
garbanzo beans

¼ cup olive oil

2 Tbsp lemon juice

¼ tsp garlic powder

¼ tsp salt

Pita bread

Tip

*There are lots of fun
ways to eat hummus.
Try it on pretzels, fresh
veggies—even bagels!*

Wondrous Homemade Hummus

Flavored with lemon and garlic, this tasty chickpea spread is a snack fit for royalty.

Directions

1. Drain the garbanzo beans and combine with the olive oil, lemon juice, garlic powder, and salt in the bowl of a food processor or blender.

2. Blend ingredients until smooth.

3. Spoon the hummus into a small bowl. Serve with pita bread triangles.

Enchanting Strawberry Roses

A rose began Belle and the Beast's tale. Relive the story by making these beautiful edible roses.

Directions

1. Wash the strawberries in cold water and pat them dry with a paper towel.

2. Ask an adult to help you with the knife. Then, slice off the strawberries' leafy tops.

3. Turn one of the strawberries upside down. Create an outer row of 4 rose petals around the tip by slicing three-quarters of the way down through the berry on all 4 sides.

4. To finish the rose, cut a second strawberry in half from top to bottom. Then cut one of the halves into several slices. Tuck 3 or 4 of the slices between the tip and outer petals of the first berry.

5. Repeat with the remaining strawberries. Store any leftover strawberry pieces in the refrigerator to enjoy as a snack later.

6. Put a spoonful of whipped cream into the bottoms of four small bowls. Set the strawberry roses on top, and serve.

Serves 4

Ingredients

8 large strawberries
Whipped cream

Tip

A strawberry rose makes the perfect topping for a bowl of yogurt, too.

Starfish Dip

These sea-inspired mouthfuls are quick to whip up and are especially yummy after a busy day of swimming or playing in the sand!

Ingredients

1 (10-oz) package frozen spinach, thawed

½ cup low-fat mayonnaise

1 package onion soup mix

1 (8-oz) container low-fat sour cream

2 cucumbers, sliced into 1-inch rounds

½ red pepper, cut into 1-inch-thick strips and then sliced on the diagonal

½ green pepper, cut into 1-inch-thick strips and then sliced on the diagonal

Tip

Feeling adventurous? Try putting this dip on top of other veggies and snacks, too!

Directions

1. Squeeze the spinach to remove any excess water. Put the spinach, mayonnaise, onion soup mix, and sour cream into a large bowl and combine.

2. Using the back of a small spoon, smear about a teaspoon of dip onto one side of a cucumber round. Arrange 5 pieces of pepper to give the appearance of a starfish, and serve.

Towering Parfaits

After discovering the world outside her tower, Rapunzel is very happy she left. Still, it's fun to remember her old home with this tasty treat's towering layers of pudding, fruit, and whipped cream.

Directions

1. Spoon a little pudding into the bottoms of two parfait glasses. Top the pudding with a layer of fresh berries, followed by a big dollop of whipped cream.

2. Repeat step 1.

3. Add one more layer of pudding.

4. Top each parfait with a small blob of whipped cream garnished with 1 or 2 fresh berries.

Makes 2

Ingredients

Lemon or vanilla low-fat pudding

Fresh blueberries or blackberries

Whipped cream

Tip

For another yummy version of this snack, you can make this treat with yogurt instead of pudding.

Beverages

Ingredients

1 qt water

3 bags herbal
raspberry tea

2 bags herbal mint tea

2 or 3 Tbsp honey
(optional)

Ice

Tip

*Just about any
flavor of fruit tea
works well with
this recipe.*

Raspberry Mint Iced Tea

Mrs. Potts is known for her delicious tea. But once you've brewed this recipe, your skills might rival even hers!

Directions

1. Ask an adult for help at the stove. Heat the water in a teapot until it is near boiling. Then remove from heat.

2. Steep the bags of raspberry and mint tea in the water for 4 minutes.

3. Remove the tea bags and stir in the honey (if adding) while the tea is still warm. Let the sweetened tea cool.

4. Fill tall glasses with plenty of ice, pour in the tea, and serve.

Sun Punch

This golden-yellow drink is as sparkly as the floating lanterns that light the sky on Rapunzel's birthday.

Directions

1. Stir the lemonade and orange juice together in a pitcher.

2. Slowly pour in the seltzer water.

3. Fill four tall glasses with plenty of ice. Pour in the punch, and serve.

Serves 4

Ingredients

1 cup lemonade

1 cup orange juice

2 cups seltzer water

Ice

Tip

For a festive touch, add a slice of orange or lemon to each glass.

Sweet Sea-Foam Smoothie

Ingredients

1 banana

½ cup water

1 cup vanilla frozen yogurt

1 Tbsp lime juice

Tip

For a sweet switch, try making this smoothie with fresh-squeezed lemon or orange juice instead of lime juice.

Flavored with lime and banana, this frothy smoothie will remind you of ocean waves.

Directions

1. Break the banana into pieces and put them into a blender.

2. Add the water, frozen yogurt, and lime juice.

3. Blend the ingredients until they are smooth and creamy.

4. Pour the smoothie into a tall glass, and serve with a straw.

White Hot Chocolate

Even Snow White gets chilly in the winter! This sweet and creamy white cocoa will warm you up in no time.

Directions

1. Ask an adult to help you at the stove. Mix the white chocolate chips and light cream in a small heavy saucepan. Warm the mixture over low heat, stirring the whole time, until the chips melt.

2. Stir in the milk and vanilla extract. Continue stirring until the mixture is warm but not too hot. Remove the pan from the heat.

3. Whisk the white hot chocolate to make it foamy on top.

4. Spoon the foam into two large cups or mugs. Then slowly pour in the rest of the hot chocolate. Sprinkle a little cinnamon or nutmeg on top, and serve.

Serves 2

Ingredients

⅓ cup white chocolate chips

⅓ cup light cream

1½ cups milk

½ tsp vanilla extract

Dash of cinnamon or nutmeg

Tip

During the holiday season, add a hint of mint by serving this drink with candy cane stirrers.

Te Fiti Tropical Punch

Serves 12

Ingredients

3 cups blue tropical punch

1 cup pineapple juice

1 cup orange juice

Lime slices, blueberries, and mint for garnishing

Tip

Double the recipe if needed to fill your pitcher.

After Moana bravely restored Te Fiti's heart, Te Fiti healed the dying land in a beautiful burst of color. This punch's bright hues take inspiration from that enchanting moment.

Directions

1. Combine the punch, pineapple juice, and orange juice in a large pitcher.

2. To serve, pour into a glass filled with ice. Garnish with a slice of lime, a few blueberries, and a sprig of mint.

Sweets

Tiger-Stripe Fudge

As far as tigers go, Rajah is truly one of a kind. Not only is he protective and loyal, he also has a unique pattern of stripes. That's why this striped fudge is so much fun to make—it turns out a little different every time!

Directions

1. Heavily grease an 8- or 9-inch square pan, then line it with parchment paper.

2. Measure the semisweet chocolate chips into a small microwavable bowl or cup. Set aside for now.

3. Ask an adult to help you at the stove. Combine the sweetened condensed milk and white chocolate chips in a nonstick frying pan. Heat over medium heat, stirring continually until the chips are completely melted.

4. Add the butterscotch chips, and turn the heat down to medium-low. Continue to heat and stir the mixture until the chips are melted. Remove the pan from the heat.

5. Add the vanilla extract, stirring until the mixture is smooth and glossy. Ask an adult to help you carefully pour the butterscotch into the prepared pan.

6. Immediately microwave the chocolate chips for 30 seconds. Stir the heated chips into a smooth sauce. The chips will not lose their shape until you do this. Quickly stir half-and-half into the melted chocolate so that it will be liquid enough to pour.

7. Drizzle spoonfuls of the melted chocolate in long lines on top of the butterscotch. Next, use the edge of a butter knife to swirl or crisscross the fudge a few times. Don't overdo it, or the two colors will mix together.

8. Chill the fudge until it sets up enough to slice (about 2 to 3 hours). Lift the ends of the parchment paper to remove the fudge from the pan. Peel off the paper, and slice the fudge into 2-inch pieces.

♕ ♕ ♕
• • •

Makes 2¼ lbs

Ingredients

¼ cup semisweet chocolate chips

1 (14-oz) can sweetened condensed milk

1 (11-oz) bag white chocolate chips

1 (11-oz) bag butterscotch chips

1 tsp vanilla extract

3 tsp half-and-half

Tip

You can use metal cookie cutters to cut the fudge into fun shapes instead of squares.

113

Ingredients

2 flour tortillas
1 Tbsp butter, melted
Colored sugar

Tip

You can't go wrong decorating a magic wand. Try this recipe with cinnamon sugar!

Bibbidi-Bobbidi-Boo Magic Wands

The phrase "bibbidi-bobbidi-boo" may sound like gibberish, but when Cinderella's fairy godmother says it and waves her wand, all kinds of incredible things start to happen. These sugar-sprinkled wands may just spread a little magic, too.

Directions

1. Heat the oven to 375°F. Line a baking sheet with parchment paper.

2. Use kitchen scissors to cut the tortillas into long ¾-inch-wide strips.

3. Ask an adult to help you with the oven. Arrange the strips on the parchment paper, and bake them for 2 minutes. With a spatula, flip the strips over and bake them for 1 or 2 more minutes.

4. Use a pastry brush to lightly coat each baked wand with melted butter, and then sprinkle on a pinch or two of colored sugar.

Apple Dumplings

Snow White would never let one bad experience with an apple keep her from enjoying such a delicious fruit! This apple dumpling recipe doesn't cast any magic spells, but it will still enchant you.

Directions

1. Heat the oven to 375°F. Butter an 8- or 9-inch square glass baking pan.

2. To make the dough, whisk together the flour, baking powder, salt, and nutmeg in a mixing bowl. Cut the butter into small pieces, and use your fingertips to pinch them into the flour mixture until the lumps are the size of peas. Stir the milk into the flour mixture.

3. Turn the dough onto a floured surface, and knead it several times so that it holds together. Dust the top of the dough with flour, and then roll it into a 12-inch square.

4. Cut the dough into four equal squares. Place 2 apple quarters and one piece of butter on each square.

5. In a small bowl, mix together the brown sugar, cinnamon, and nutmeg. Spoon the mixture onto the apples, dividing it equally between the dumplings.

6. To finish each dumpling, moisten the edges of the dough with water. Then, gather the dough corners together on top of the apple pieces and pinch them together. Place the dumplings in the pan, spaced about 1 inch apart.

7. Combine the syrup ingredients together in a small pitcher. Stir well, and pour the syrup into the pan with the dumplings. Ask an adult to help you with the oven. Bake the dumplings for 20 to 25 minutes, until the tops are golden brown and the apples tender.

8. Allow the dumplings to cool for a few minutes. Then spoon some syrup over the top, and serve.

Serves 4

Ingredients

Dough
1½ cups flour

1 tsp baking powder

½ tsp salt

¼ tsp nutmeg

3 Tbsp cold butter

½ cup milk

Filling
2 peeled apples, cored and cut into quarters

1 Tbsp butter, cut into quarters

3 Tbsp brown sugar

¼ tsp cinnamon

¼ tsp nutmeg

Syrup
1 cup hot water

½ cup packed brown sugar

2 Tbsp butter, melted

Tip

Firm apples, like Granny Smiths, Jonathans, or Red Romes, work especially well for this recipe.

Ingredients

1 dozen frosted cupcakes

2 Tbsp extra frosting

24 green gumdrops

12 sour apple gummy ring candies

12 spearmint leaf gummy candies

24 mini chocolate chips

Tip

Instead of mini chocolate chips, you can use candy eyeballs or draw eyes yourself with an edible-ink marker.

Sea Turtle Cupcakes

Ariel might live on land now, but she's always thinking of her sea creature friends. Bring a bit more sea to land with these adorable cupcakes!

Directions

1. Ask an adult to help you with a knife. For each cupcake, make a candy turtle shell by cutting a gumdrop in half horizontally. Use a small dab of frosting to stick the top half of the gumdrop to the center of a gummy ring. Set the shell in the middle of the cupcake top, pressing down slightly to stick it in place.

2. For fins, set a spearmint leaf candy on a cutting board and slice it in half lengthwise.

3. Set one of the halves on its side, cut side down, and slice it in half down the middle to make two thinner pieces. Do the same with the other half of the candy. Set two pieces in place on the cupcake for the turtle's front flippers, and use the remaining two pieces for the back flippers.

4. For the turtle's head, apply a tiny dab of frosting to the back of a mini chocolate chip. Then stick the "eyeball" to the upper right side of a gumdrop. Attach another mini chocolate chip to the opposite side of the gumdrop.

5. Set the gumdrop head on the cupcake at the front of the shell, gently pressing the very bottom portion into the frosting to stick it in place.

Dreamy Carrot Cookies

Prince Phillip's horse, Samson, can be stubborn at times, but he never shies away from helping Aurora. Filled with carrots, oats, and apples, these colorful cookies take inspiration from a horse's favorite treats.

Directions

1. Heat the oven to 375°F. Line a baking sheet with parchment paper.

2. In a small bowl, whisk together the flour, baking powder, salt, cinnamon, and nutmeg.

3. In a large bowl, stir together the brown sugar and melted butter. Then, beat in the egg with a fork.

4. Stir the flour mixture into the sugar mixture until the batter is smooth. Then stir in the oats, shredded carrot and apple, walnuts, and cranberries.

5. Drop rounded tablespoons of batter onto the cookie sheet, spacing them about ½ inch apart.

6. Ask an adult to help you with the oven. Bake the cookies until they just begin to turn golden brown on top, about 8 minutes. Leave them on the baking sheet for 2 minutes before moving them to a wire rack to cool.

7. Repeat steps 5 and 6 until you've baked all the batter.

Ingredients

1 cup flour

1 tsp baking powder

½ tsp salt

½ tsp cinnamon

½ tsp nutmeg

½ cup brown sugar

¼ cup melted butter

1 egg, lightly beaten

1 cup rolled oats

1 cup shredded carrot

½ cup shredded apple

½ cup chopped walnuts

⅓ cup dried cranberries

Tip

In a pinch, you can use raisins instead of dried cranberries.

Toasted Oatmeal Ice Cream

Serves 4

Ingredients

2 tsp maple syrup

¾ tsp canola oil

⅛ tsp cinnamon

Dash of salt

3 Tbsp rolled oats

1 pint vanilla ice cream

Tip

You can stir in other mix-ins, such as chocolate chips, chopped walnuts, or even crushed berries, along with the toasted oats.

Merida's horse, Angus, loves to munch on raw oats. But for a delicious treat fit for a human, try mixing them in ice cream with this tasty cinnamon syrup.

Directions

1. In a small bowl, stir together the maple syrup, canola oil, cinnamon, and salt. Set the mixture aside.

2. Ask an adult to help you at the stove. Heat the oats in a small nonstick frying pan over low heat. Stir them gently with a wooden spoon until they are lightly toasted (about 3 minutes).

3. Remove the pan from the heat, and pour in the maple syrup mixture. Quickly stir the oats until they are evenly coated and the syrup stops sizzling. Let the oats cool in the pan for a couple of minutes, then spread them on a tray to finish cooling.

4. Take the ice cream out of the freezer and let it thaw for a few minutes. As soon as it's soft enough, spoon it into a small mixing bowl.

5. Use a wooden spoon to stir the cooled toasted oats into the ice cream. Then spoon the ice cream back into the container, and return it to the freezer. When the ice cream has hardened up again, it's ready to serve.

Monkey Bread

Sometimes it takes a little convincing to get Jasmine's friend Abu to share his bread. With this sweet and sticky pull-apart treat, there's plenty for everybody!

Directions

1. Heat the oven to 375°F. Generously grease a nonstick fluted tube pan.

2. In a mixing bowl, stir together the flour, baking powder, and salt. With a table knife, cut the butter into small pieces. Use your fingertips to pinch the butter into the flour mixture until the lumps of butter are about the size of peas. Then stir in the milk.

3. Turn the dough onto a floured surface and knead it for about 5 seconds. Pull off pieces of the dough and shape them into 2½ to 3 dozen golf-ball-size pieces.

4. Mix the brown sugar, white sugar, and cinnamon together in a small bowl.

5. One at a time, dip the dough balls into the melted butter, roll them in the sugar mixture, and place them in the prepared pan. Stack the balls on top of one another until the pan is full.

6. Ask an adult to help you with the oven. Bake the monkey bread for 20 to 25 minutes. You can tell if the bread is ready by sticking a toothpick into it. If the toothpick comes out clean, the bread is done baking. Set the bread aside to cool for about 10 minutes.

7. Use a small spatula to gently loosen the bread from the sides of the pan. Now it's time to turn the monkey bread out of the pan. Be sure to ask an adult for help with this step! First, place a serving dish facedown on top of the fluted tube pan. Next, hold the dish and pan together securely, and flip them over. Slowly lift the pan off the plate and release the monkey bread.

8. Let the bread cool slightly. Then pull pieces from it, and enjoy!

Serves 8 to 10

Ingredients

3 cups flour

4 tsp baking powder

1 tsp salt

⅓ cup cold butter

1¼ cups milk

½ cup brown sugar

½ cup white sugar

1 tsp cinnamon

6 Tbsp butter, melted

Tip

For an even sweeter dessert, top some monkey bread with a scoop of ice cream.

Princess Pink Popcorn

As far as the good fairy Flora is concerned, everything looks pretty in pink. Why not add a dash of pink to your popcorn, too?

Ingredients

Bag of popped microwave popcorn (about 6 cups)

2½ Tbsp butter

18 large marshmallows

3 Tbsp strawberry-flavored gelatin powder

Tip

Melted marshmallow is hot, so be sure to use a long-handled spoon to stir it.

Directions

1. Put the popped popcorn in a large mixing bowl, removing any unpopped kernels.

2. Ask an adult to help you at the stove. Melt the butter in a medium-size saucepan over medium-low heat. Add the marshmallows and stir continually until they melt and turn into a smooth sauce. Stir in the strawberry gelatin powder. Use a plastic spoon for this step. (The pink gelatin can stain a wooden spoon.)

3. Immediately pour the pink marshmallow sauce over the popcorn, and gently stir to evenly cover the kernels.

4. Let the popcorn cool for a few minutes before serving.

Magical Menus

On their own, each of these recipes is a delicious treat, but add a few dishes together and you get a complete feast! Take a look at these magical menus that combine a few different Disney Princess–inspired dishes. Then try creating your own.

Head Start Brunch

Frying Pan Eggs
24

Baked Caramel
French Toast
28

Raspberry Mint
Iced Tea
100

Midday Feast

Bull's-Eye Pizza
44

All-Dressed-Up
Salad
78

Sun Punch
102

Winter Warm-Up Lunch

Castle Corn Chowder
32

Cozy Cottage Chicken
Tenders
50

White Hot
Chocolate
106

Summer Picnic

Tasty Flower
Sandwiches
40

Lucky Cucumber Salad
66

Sweet Sea-Foam
Smoothie
104

Magical Princess Party

Magic Carpet Roll-Ups
38

Enchanting
Strawberry Roses
92

Bibbidi-Bobbidi-Boo
Magic Wands
114

Family Dinner

Bayou Meatloaf

58

Sweet Potato Coins

70

Dinglehopper
Snow Peas

82

Glossary

A

Al dente—an Italian term used to describe pastas or vegetables that are still firm (instead of soft or mushy) when you're done cooking them. Foods prepared al dente are usually more flavorful than foods that cook longer.

B

Baguette—a long, narrow loaf of French bread with a crisp crust

Bake—to cook ingredients in an oven

Baking sheet—a flat metal pan for baking cookies, biscuits, or breads

Beat—to quickly stir an ingredient or batter with a whisk, electric mixer, or spoon until it is smooth and/or fluffy

Blend—to combine two or more ingredients into a smooth mixture

C

Casserole dish—a glass or ceramic dish used for cooking and serving foods

Celery salt—a flavored salt made with ground celery seeds

Chop—to cut an ingredient into pieces that are roughly the same size

Cream—to blend ingredients, typically butter and sugar, into a soft and creamy mixture

Crumbled—broken or rubbed into small pieces

D

Dash—a small amount of an ingredient, such as lemon juice or cinnamon, added to a recipe from the container with a quick shake of the wrist

Dice—to cut foods into small cubes (typically ¼ inch wide)

Dill weed—a sweet herb harvested from the flowering tops of dill plants

Drizzle—to slowly pour a thin stream of liquid or a melted ingredient over another food

Dust—to lightly sprinkle a powdery ingredient, such as confectioners' sugar or flour. Rolling pins are often dusted with flour to keep them from sticking to piecrust, cookie dough, or other foods that are rolled out.

E

Extract—a concentrated flavoring made by soaking certain foods, such as vanilla beans, in water and/or other liquids

F

Fillet—a piece of fish or meat from which the bones have been removed

Flake—to break a piece of food, such as cooked fish, into smaller pieces with a fork

Fold—to gently blend ingredients by using a spatula to cut through the middle of the batter and then flip the left half of the batter over onto the right half. Stiff beaten egg whites are often folded, rather than stirred, into cake and soufflé recipes to keep as much air in the batter as possible.

G

Garbanzo beans—round tan beans, also called chickpeas, with a mild nutty flavor

Garnish—to decorate a prepared recipe with an herb, fruit, or other edible ingredient that adds color and/or texture

Grate—to shred foods, such as coconut, carrots, cheese, or chocolate, into bits or flakes by rubbing them against a grater

Ground—when a dry ingredient has been broken up into very small pieces, often with a powderlike texture

K

Knead—to repeatedly fold and press together dough until it is smooth and stretchy. Kneading traps air bubbles produced by the yeast, which is what makes the dough rise.

M

Mandarin orange—a small citrus fruit with a sweeter taste than a regular orange has.

Mince—to chop ingredients, such as garlic cloves, gingerroot, or fresh herbs, extra fine. This evenly distributes the flavor in the dish you are cooking.

P

Paprika—a spice made from ground dried bell or chili peppers

Parchment paper—heat-resistant paper used to line a baking sheet so cookies and other foods won't stick to the pan when you bake them

Pat—to gently tap dough with the palm of your hand

Pie shell—unbaked pie dough that is molded into a pie tin, then baked with the pie filling

Pinch—a small amount of a dry ingredient, such as salt or a ground spice, added to a recipe with your fingertips

Pita bread—a flat, round bread made without yeast

Produce—fresh fruits and vegetables

Puree—to blend food until it is completely smooth

R

Rice vinegar—a vinegar made from fermented rice wine. Popular in China, this type of vinegar has a much sweeter taste than Western vinegars.

S

Saucepan—a deep pan with a long handle and a cover that is meant for cooking foods on a stovetop

Sauté—to quickly cook food on the stovetop in a lightly oiled pan

Scramble—to stir and/or break food, such as eggs or hamburger, into small bits while it cooks

Seltzer water—water that has been

combined with carbon dioxide, making it bubbly

Separate egg whites—to divide egg whites from their yolks. To do this, remove the top half of the eggshell so that both the yolk and white are still in the bottom half. Working over the bowl, slide the yolk from one half of the shell to the other, letting the egg white fall into the bowl underneath. Pour the yolk into a separate bowl.

Shallot—a type of onion with a mild flavor

Shred—to pull or cut an ingredient into many thin strips

Simmer—to cook food on the stovetop in liquid heated just to the point at which small bubbles rise to the surface

Snip—to use kitchen scissors to cut an ingredient into small pieces

Soften—to warm butter (either by setting it out at room temperature or heating it in a microwave) until it is easy to combine with a mixture

Sprig—a small piece of an herb, usually including the full stem

Strain—to remove the liquid from food by pouring it into a colander, metal sieve, or cheesecloth. The juice or broth passes through the sieve and the solids are retained.

Sweetened condensed milk—milk that has been mixed with sugar and simmered until half or more of the water in it has evaporated and the remaining liquid is thick and creamy

T

To taste—just enough of a certain ingredient, usually salt, to improve the flavor of a recipe

W

Whip—to beat air into an ingredient, such as cream or egg whites, until it is light and fluffy

Whisk—a long-handled kitchen utensil with a series of wire or plastic loops at the end used to rapidly beat eggs, cream, or other liquids. *Whisk* is also a verb that means "to use a whisk."

Index